$20.00

D1408386

From Lands of the Night

Tololwa M. Mollel
Illustrated by Darrell McCalla

Red Deer PRESS

One day he was well. The next he had grown ill — very ill. We tried everything. We took him from one hospital to another. We prayed for him. But my baby brother grew only worse.

Then we took him to a healer.

The healer looked over Samson's wasted body and into his eyes. Then he said to me, "Only the ancestors can save your baby brother, little girl." He told my parents, "Hold a ceremony to honor your ancestors and ask for help, a joyful ceremony filled with guests."

"Joyful?" my mother said. "How can we be joyful at a time like this?"

"A joyful ceremony it must be," replied the healer. "Nothing less will bring the ancestors from their lands of the night. Let's seek joy in hope. I'll spread word of the ceremony".

On the day of the ceremony, friends, neighbors, and relatives help out. Delicious smells of cooking fill the air. By trucks, vans, scooters, bicycles, and foot, guests pour into our yard. Throbbing music drowns out the city sounds.

Big drums, *kutum-kutum-kutum-kutum antu-pom*

Smaller ones, *patap-patap-patap-patap-tururu-*

Flutes, *tiit-tiit-tiit-tiit-tiit-*

Xylophones, *gidi-gidi-gidi-gidi-godo-*

And singers, *aaae-aaae aaae-aaae!*

My father wanders through the crowd. He makes sure all have
enough to eat and drink. My youngest aunt — I call her Little Aunt —
is in the house helping my mother. Samson has grown even worse.
I am dressed colorfully and my hair is freshly braided.
I stand at the gate of our compound to help
welcome people.

Darkness brings strange guests.

An old man whose ears remind me of a hare. Two shy girls who look like nymphs. A dancing giant of a man in a mask. An old woman whose dress shimmers and winks with stars. My father, stopping, leans down and speaks in my ear. "They come from lands of the night, Ra-Eli. The healer spread word, indeed."

Just then, out of the night appears the strangest guest. She shakes her head when I welcome her. She announces "It's not for the ceremony that I've come. I've been sent. By Mola."

I stare at the angel. "By . . . God?"

"Yes. God — Mola. Mola says your music is too loud. Mola can't rest, can't think. Mola sent me to ask: could you kindly stop?"

I tell the angel about Samson, and about the ancestors. And then I ask, "Would you please be our guest?"

The music has stopped. The angel hesitates but, as we all watch, my father, most graciously, leads her to a seat in the yard.

She sits down politely, but she's not smiling.

From the midst of the crowd, I admire the angel. I like her bangles and earrings. Her neat braids are jet-black and glossy — like mine. I have questions I wish to ask but music, loud and magical, soon fills the night again.

kutum-kutum-kutum-kutum antu-pom

patap-patap-patap-patap tururu-

tiit-tiit-tiit-tiit-tiit-

gidi-gidi-gidi-gidi-godo-

aaae-aaae aaae-aaae!

The angel watches and listens. Slowly, her fingers begin to drum on her knee, turu . . . turu, to the music, turu . . . turu . . . turu. She sways her shoulders. She taps her foot, kop . . . kop . . . kop. Then she looks up in surprise when dancers approach and ask her to dance.

Smiling, she gets to her feet.

More guests come, followed by another angel! Before I can welcome this other angel, the dancers skip up. The second angel pulls back startled but, watching the dancers, he's moved to dance too — first in small modest steps, then gradually in bolder motions, more and more joyfully, his long white hair flowing about.

One after another, more angels appear. One after another, all are moved to dance. Music sprays into the night, louder than ever.

Kutum-kutum-kutum-kutum antu-pom

patap-patap-patap-

A burst of light from a lamp brings the ceremony to a stop.

The dazzling light turns night into day. City sounds fade away.
In the complete hush, we blink in awe and astonishment.

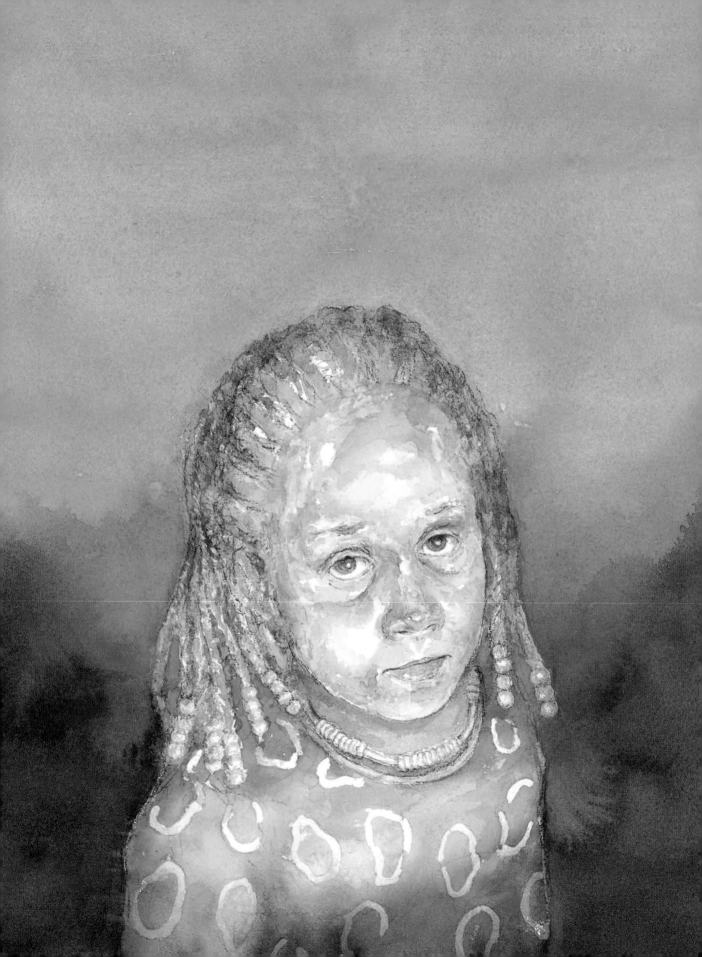

The light dims. Night creeps back. Sounds slowly return. Mola, at the gate, speaks. "What on earth do you all think you're doing? I have much work and thinking to do, but how can I with your loud music? All I want is some peace, some quiet, to rest, so I can think. Again and again I sent word asking you to stop. I've come to ask you myself."

I inch closer to the Mola. I say, "We're having . . . a ceremony . . . for my . . . baby brother." Mola turns, casting a circle of light around me. I tell Mola about Samson and about the ancestors.

I reach out to Mola. "Would you please . . . be our . . . guest?"

Mola stares at me, and around at the sea of eyes watching.

We watch and wait. I hope Mola says yes. We watch and wait. We wait . . . until, slowly moved, Mola at last also reaches out.

I take Mola's hand.

And I'm surprised how small it is. Smaller, even, than mine! Not at all what I imagined God would look like: the hands so young, yet the face so . . . old . . . and — funny thing — the color, exactly, of my copper earrings!

I lead Mola to a seat. And music starts again.

kutum-kutum-kutum-kutum antu-pom

patap-patap-patap-patap tururu-

tiit-tiit-tiit-tiit-tiit-

gidi-gidi-gidi-gidi-godo-

aaae-aaae aaae-aaae!

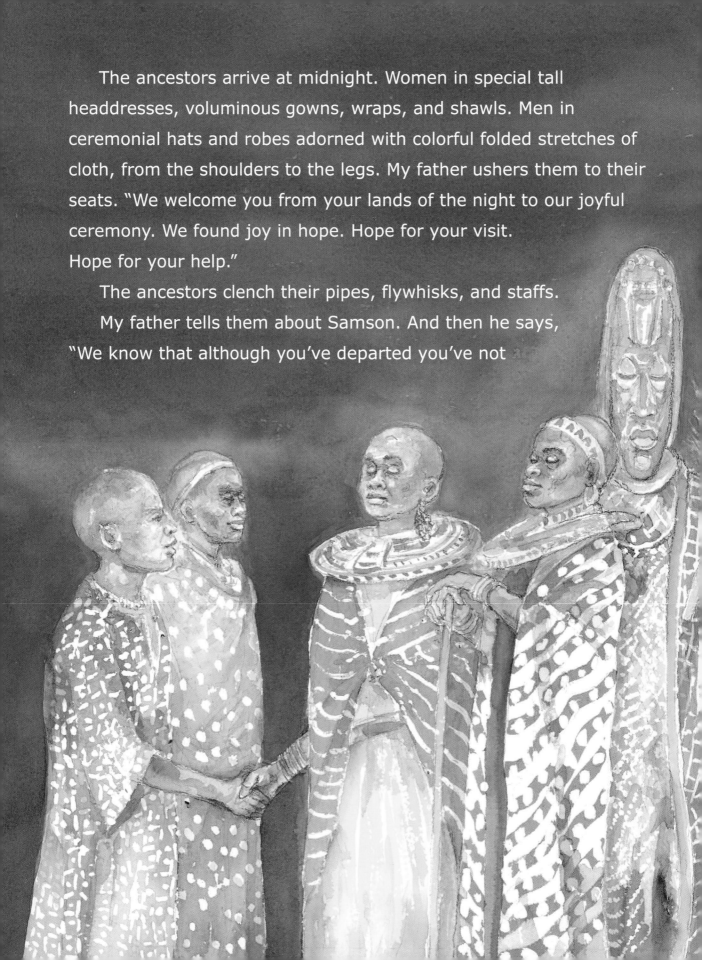

The ancestors arrive at midnight. Women in special tall headdresses, voluminous gowns, wraps, and shawls. Men in ceremonial hats and robes adorned with colorful folded stretches of cloth, from the shoulders to the legs. My father ushers them to their seats. "We welcome you from your lands of the night to our joyful ceremony. We found joy in hope. Hope for your visit. Hope for your help."

The ancestors clench their pipes, flywhisks, and staffs.

My father tells them about Samson. And then he says, "We know that although you've departed you've not abandoned us, and that in time of need we can call on you and you can help. Tonight we hope that you will."

My mother addresses the ancestors next. Then my grandmothers do. Followed by my grandfather, my uncles and aunts, and other relatives. Then we all place gifts at the feet of the ancestors. Tobacco, honey, tea leaves, cloth, overcoats, hats, blankets, mirrors, and handkerchiefs.

When we finish, my mother sends me to stay with Samson.

"And get some sleep, Ra-Eli," she says. "You're very tired."

In the house, I slip into bed beside Samson. He's asleep but restless and damp. He struggles to breathe. Little Aunt, who was minding him, leaves for the ceremony.

I pat Samson while the ceremony continues.

Kutum-kutum-kutum-kutum antu-pom,
patap-patap-patap-patap tururu . . . !

I fall asleep despite the music . . .

. . . but snap awake after what seems only a short time! Then I realize how long I've slept: the ceremony is over. Suddenly in the silence, I notice something else, something that causes me to spring out of bed. My mother, who has been sleeping in another bed, wakes up too. "What's the matter?"

I tell her. "Samson is not in bed!"

My mother gets up. I turn on the light. "He's nowhere to be seen." But I continue to look around

My mother says, "Listen." I do, and I too hear the voices . . . low, coming from the yard. I follow my mother as she heads quickly out.

In the yard, we step between guests asleep all over the ground and edge toward the gate. There, in a circle, stand the ancestors, the angels — and Mola. We watch them hum and chant, hum and chant, hum and chant, while they pass a swaddled baby around to one another. I sink to my knees at the awesome sight — I just do, I don't know why. On and on in the quiet dawn, they pass around the baby and hum and chant, time and again.

When they finally finish, Mola turns and shuffling from the circle, brings Samson to where we are and into my mother's arms.

"Here."

One evening, weeks after the ceremony, my mother and I sat on our veranda. She was taking out my hairbraids. Samson crawled tirelessly about. I got up when he tried to go down the steps to the yard. He protested when I lifted him but stopped to watch when I whispered, "Look, look . . . " and pointed out oddly shaped clouds and the moon low in the sky. Samson giggled as I cheered on the clouds drifting across the moon one after another.

Behind us, my mother approached.

She took Samson from me and we all gazed at the lands of the night. As we did, I thought of the night of the ceremony. That distant throbbing night of hope. Our hope that was now fulfilled.

To Samson's excitement, I danced.

kutum-kutum-kutum-kutum antu-pom

patap-patap-patap-patap tururu-

tiit-tiit-tiit-tiit-tiit-

gidi-gidi-gidi-gidi-godo-

aaae-aaae aaae-aaae!

Dedication

In memory of our son and brother, Leseriani Mollel. — Tololwa

To Brianna and Dominique, for the emotion and laughter. — Darrell

Author's Note

Many cultures believe that when people die they turn over time into ancestors, our forefathers and foremothers. We don't see these ancestors but they exist, we are told, mysteriously, some-where. In this story they exist in "lands of the night." People believe that ancestors possess powers to assist the living during difficult times. To get such help, people at times ask a special person, like the healer in this story, to connect them with the ancestors.

Christianity and Islam normally discourage belief in the powers of the ancestors to help the living. But many Christians and Moslems, and people who are neither, still hold this belief. This is the case in many African countries. It's also the case in countries like Brazil and Haiti that have big populations descended from Africa. These countries mix Christianity and belief in the helping powers of the ancestors in their cultures. Such a mix also exists to this day in the East African country of Tanzania, where I grew up. This mix has always fascinated me. It's what led me to create this story. My final inspiration for the story came from a tale in Harold Courlander's collection, *The Piece of Fire and Other Haitian Tales*.

Published in Canada by Red Deer Press
195 Allstate Parkway, Markham, ON, L3R 4T8
www.reddeerpress.com

Published in the U.S. by Red Deer Press
311 Washington Street, Brighton, Massachusetts 02135

Edited for the Press by Peter Carver
Cover and text design by Blair Kerrigan/Glyphics
Printed and bound in China by Sheck Wah Tong Printing Press Ltd.

5 4 3 2 1

We acknowledge with thanks the Canada Council for the Arts, and the Ontario Arts Council for their support of our publishing program. We acknowledge the financial support of the Government of Canada through the Canada Book Fund (CBF) for our publishing activities.

Canada Council for the Arts   Conseil des Arts du Canada

ONTARIO ARTS COUNCIL
CONSEIL DES ARTS DE L'ONTARIO

Library and Archives Canada Cataloguing in Publication
Mollel, Tololwa M. (Tololwa Marti), author
        From lands of the night / Tololwa M. Mollel ; illustrated by Darrell McCalla.
ISBN 978-0-88995-498-4 (bound)
        I. McCalla, Darrell, illustrator II. Title.
PS8576.O451F76 2013   jC813'.54   C2013-906403-6

Publisher Cataloging-in-Publication Data (U.S.)
Mollel, Tololwa M.
        From lands of the night / Tololwa M. Mollel ; Darrell McCalla.
[32] p. : col. ill. ; cm.
Summary: A young girl watches as her family agonizes over the illness of her baby brother. They approach a healer, and what follows is a true testament to the power of ceremony and music and the honoring of ancestors.
ISBN-13: 978-0-88995-498-4 (pbk.)
1. Healing – Juvenile fiction. 2. Brothers and sisters – Juvenile fiction. 3. Rites and ceremonies – Juvenile fiction. I. McCalla, Darrell. II. Title.
[Fic] dc23   PZ7.M6554Fr   2013